My Lucky Hat

Kevin O'Malley

For my brother Shawn—K.O'M.

For information contact:
MONDO Publishing
980 Avenue of the Americas
New York, NY 10018

MONDO is a registered trademark of Mondo Publishing

Visit our website at
www.mondopub.com

Manufactured by Regent Publishing Services, Hong Kong
Printed May 2011 in Guangdong, China-11568
02 03 04 05 06 07 08   HC   9 8 7 6 5 4 3 2
11 12 13 14   PB   12 11 10 9

Design by Kevin O'Malley and Mina Greenstein

Library of Congress Cataloging-in-Publication Data
O'Malley, Kevin, 1961-
My lucky hat / Kevin O'Malley.
p.   cm.
Summary: When Frank's favorite baseball player, the
mighty Keefoffer, strikes out, Frank loans him his
lucky hat to help him hit a home run.
ISBN 1-57255-710-9 (hardcover : alk. paper). —
ISBN 1-57255-709-5 (pbk. : alk. paper)
[1. Baseball—Fiction.   2. Hats—Fiction.
3. Luck—Fiction.]   I. Title.
PZ7.O526My   1999
[Fic]—dc21   98-43057
CIP   AC

The illustrations were created on
lightweight cream-colored paper using
art markers and colored pencils.

"I won!" shouted Frank. "I won two tickets to the Knights game. My lucky hat did it again!"

Two days later, Frank and Dad
were at Knights Stadium.

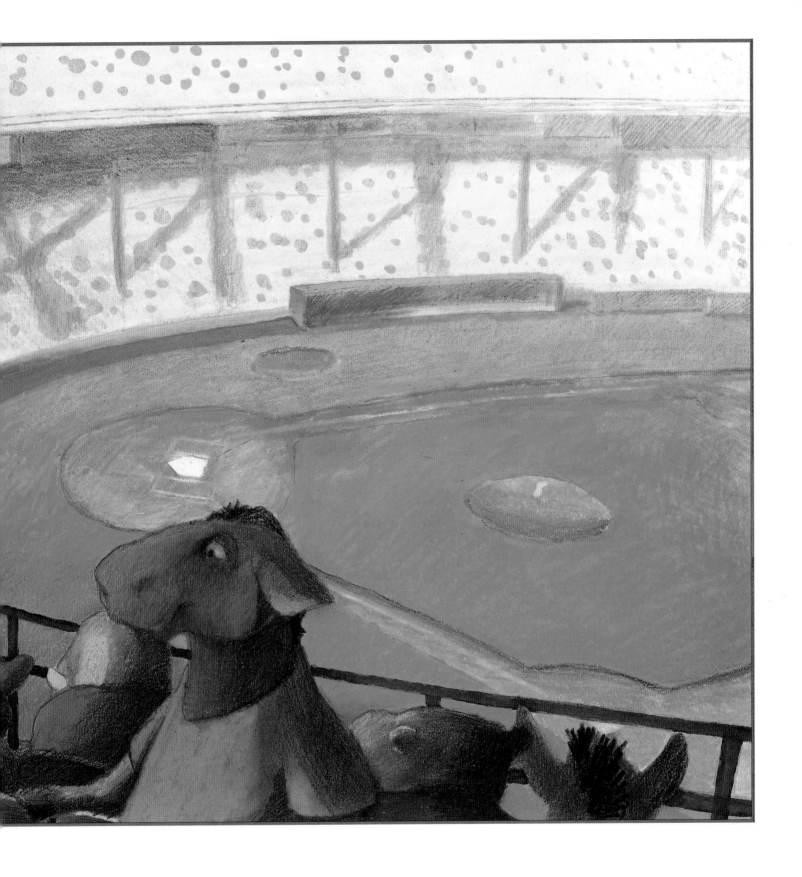

Of course, Frank was wearing
his lucky hat.

Frank watched the game anxiously.
"Come on, lucky hat," he whispered.
"Come on, lucky hat."

By the eighth inning, the Knights were
losing. Frank's favorite player, the mighty
Keefoffer, had just struck out.

"My lucky hat isn't working this time,"
Frank said sadly.

"Come on," said Dad. "Let's get something
to eat. Just smell those hot dogs. Nothing is
better at a ball game than a hot dog."

Suddenly Frank was pushed through
a door.

"FRANK!" Dad called.

Click went the door. Frank was trapped.

Frank tiptoed down the hall. All he
could hear was the *tic tic tic tic* of his
toenails on the cold, hard floor.
"Dad," he whispered. "Dad."

Frank crept down some stairs.
"Daddy," he said softly.

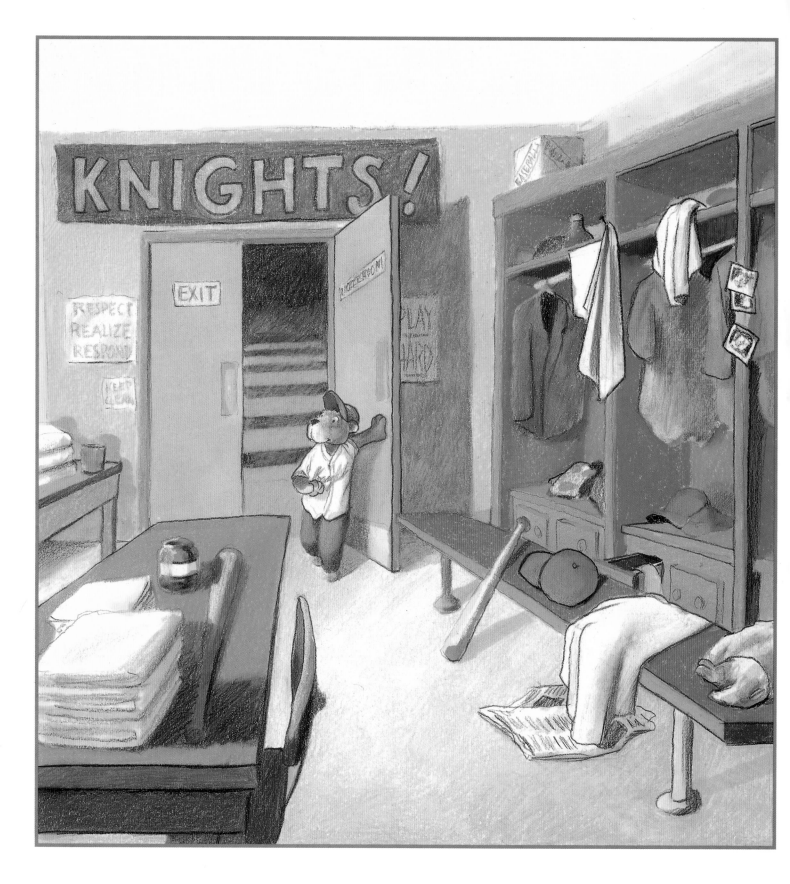

Then Frank heard a rumbling like
thunder all around him.

The rumbling grew louder and louder
as he moved toward the doors.

Frank swung open the doors.
The crowd roared in his ears.

"Wow," whispered Frank. "WOW!"

Suddenly Frank was face-to-face with
the manager.
Uh-oh, I'm in trouble now, Frank thought.

"Listen, son," said the manager. "I don't
have time for any pranks. I've got a game
to win. So just sit down and stay put. Okay?

"Keefoffer, you're up!" shouted the manager. "There are two on, two out, and it's the bottom of the ninth. Try not to strike out this time."

The crowd was shouting in rhythm.
Keefoffer was shaking like a leaf.
"Pitcher's got nothing!" yelled Frank.

STRIKE ONE!

STRRR-RIKE TWO!

"Time out!" yelled Frank.
The crowd grew absolutely quiet.

"Excuse me, Mr. Keefoffer, but
I thought maybe you would like
to try my lucky hat," said Frank.

"How lucky is your hat?" asked Keefoffer.
"You'll see," said Frank.
"PLAY BALL!" shouted the umpire.

The only thing louder than the roar
of the crowd was the sound of Keefoffer's
bat connecting with the ball.

It's GOING . . . **GOING** . . .

GONE!

"Thanks, son. Thanks a million,"
said Keefoffer.
   "Don't thank me," said Frank.
"Thank my lucky hat!"